CYNTHIA RYLANT

Mr. Putter & Tabby Turn the Page

Illustrated by

ARTHUR HOWARD

Houghton Mifflin Harcourt
Boston   New York

For Judy Rule and all the
wonderful librarians
—C.R.

Copyright © 2014 by Cynthia Rylant
Illustrations copyright © 2014 by Arthur Howard

www.hmhco.com

The illustrations in this book were done in pencil, watercolor,
and gouache on 250-gram cotton rag paper.
The text type was set in Berkeley Old Style Book.
The display type was set in Artcraft.

The Library of Congress has cataloged the hardcover edition as follows:
Rylant, Cynthia.
Mr. Putter & Tabby turn the page / Cynthia Rylant & Arthur Howard.
p. cm.
Summary: Mr. Putter and Mrs. Teaberry bring Tabby and Zeke to the library for a special story time.
[1. Books and reading—Fiction. 2. Libraries—Fiction. 3. Cats—Fiction. 4. Dogs—Fiction.]
I. Howard, Arthur, illustrator. II. Title. III. Title: Mr. Putter and Tabby turn the page.
PZ7.R982Mvm 2014
[E]—dc23
2013042822

ISBN: 978-0-15-206063-3 hardcover
ISBN: 978-0-544-58232-3 paperback

Manufactured in China
SCP 10 9 8 7 6 5 4 3 2 1
4500541418

1
Reading

2
A Mistake

3
Gusto!

4
Story Time!

5
Book Swap

1

Reading

Mr. Putter and his fine cat, Tabby,
loved quiet time.
They loved quiet baths.

They loved quiet naps.

They loved quiet thinking.

Mr. Putter and Tabby spent
their favorite quiet times reading.
Mr. Putter loved to read,
but he did not like to read alone.
He liked having someone to read to.
And Tabby was the someone.

She curled up
on Mr. Putter's lap
or on Mr. Putter's feet
or on Mr. Putter's head,

and Mr. Putter read.

They had their favorite books,
which they read over and over.
One was about a cowboy.
(Mr. Putter liked cowboys.)

One was about a rabbit.

(Tabby liked rabbits.)

One was about gardens.

(Mr. Putter and Tabby both liked gardens.)

So Mr. Putter was excited
when he saw the sign at the library.
The sign said, "Read aloud with your pet."
Well, Mr. Putter read aloud
with his pet all the time!

But the sign said something else.
It said, "Read aloud with
your pet at Story Time."
Hmmm, thought Mr. Putter.

He liked the words *story time*.
They reminded him of when he was a boy.
His teacher had read stories
aloud to the children.
Story time was a very exciting time then!

Reading did not always have to be quiet.
And what could be better than Tabby
and story time and the library?
Mr. Putter signed up.

2

A Mistake

After he signed up, Mr. Putter made a mistake.
Mr. Putter told his friend and neighbor
Mrs. Teaberry about signing up.
He forgot that Mrs. Teaberry loved anything new.
Anything.

She learned new hobbies.
She made new friends.
She cooked new food.
Mrs. Teaberry liked *new*.

But Mrs. Teaberry's good dog,
Zeke, liked new too.
He liked to find new ways of doing things.
And sometimes it got a little too exciting.
Mr. Putter was not sure about
Zeke and story time.
There might be much too much
adventure with Zeke in a library!

But it was too late now.
Mrs. Teaberry was already
looking for her library hat.

3
Gusto!

Mr. Putter thought and thought about
what story to read aloud at the library.
He thought about cowboys
and he thought about rabbits.

He did not think about gardens.

Gardens were not adventures to most people.

Gardens were an adventure to Tabby,

but that is because Tabby knew

how to make them exciting.

Mr. Putter thought and thought,
and then he picked his story.
It was a story about a bear.
"Everyone likes bear stories,"
Mr. Putter told Tabby.
"Bears are exciting."

Mr. Putter practiced his story.

He held up the book.

He turned the pages.

He read with gusto.

"Gusto makes everything more exciting,"

Mr. Putter told Tabby.

Tabby purred.

Reading was not so quiet anymore.

Reading was an adventure!

4

Story Time!

On the day of story time, Mr. Putter
and Tabby and Mrs. Teaberry and Zeke
walked to the library.
At the library, all the children
were waiting for story time.
When they saw Mr. Putter and Tabby
and Mrs. Teaberry and Zeke,
they were very excited.
Tabby purred and purred.
Zeke licked a lot of faces.

Then everyone settled in for story time.

Mrs. Teaberry read her story first.

It was a story about a dog.

And Zeke made all the sound effects.

When the dog in the story barked, Zeke barked.

When the dog in the story howled, Zeke howled.

And when the dog
in the story ran away,
Zeke ran away.
"Oops!" said Mrs. Teaberry.
"Come back, Zeke!"
called the children.
"Come back, Zeke!"
called Mrs. Teaberry.

But Zeke smelled the librarians' lunchroom.

Zeke was not coming back for a while.

Mrs. Teaberry was not worried.

Zeke always came back sooner or later.

So Mr. Putter read his bear story.

While he read (with gusto),
Tabby curled up on laps
and on feet and on heads.

When Mr. Putter said "The end,"
everyone clapped.

Then Zeke came back.
He had someone's cheese
sandwich and a different hat.
He also smelled like grapefruit juice.

Everyone was happy he had come back.
When it was time to say goodbye,
the librarian gave Mr. Putter and Mrs. Teaberry
stickers and bookmarks—free!

Mr. Putter and Mrs. Teaberry both loved free stuff.
Story time had been very exciting!

5

Book Swap

When everyone got home, they needed tea.
Reading had been so exciting
that it made them hungry.
So Mrs. Teaberry made tea
and raisin biscuits for them all.

When it was time to leave,
Mr. Putter swapped his bear book
for Mrs. Teaberry's dog book.
(He and Tabby liked dog stories.
Zeke was curious about the bear.)

That night, when everyone was tucked in,
they all had free stickers and free bookmarks
and good bedtime stories.

And Zeke loved the bear.